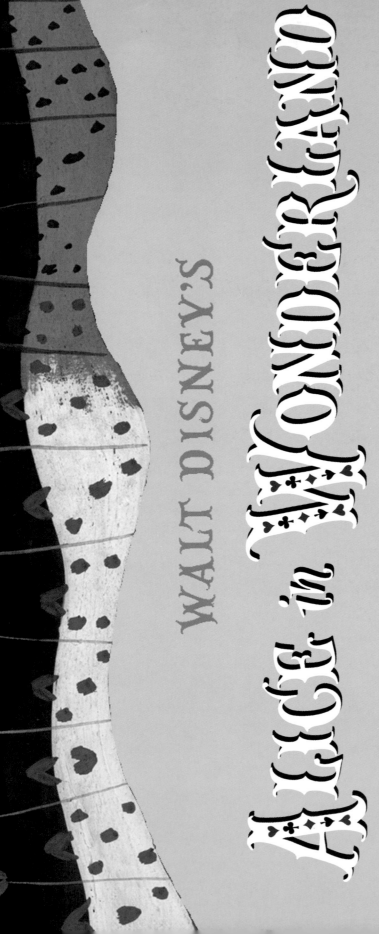

WALT DISNEY'S

Alice in Wonderland

Retold by JON SCIESZKA

Pictures by MARY BLAIR

DISNEY PRESS • NEW YORK

AN IMPRINT OF DISNEY BOOK GROUP

For Steve Malk
—J.S.

ACKNOWLEDGMENTS

Special thanks to The Walt Disney Animation Research Library staff
for their invaluable assistance and for providing all artwork
not attributed to individual collectors.

Illustration page 30: courtesy Theresa Wiseman; page 40: courtesy Kevin Blair.

"The Unbirthday Song" by Mack David, Al Hoffman, and Jerry Livingston © 1948 Walt
Disney Music Company. Used by permission.

"Painting the Roses Red" by Sammy Fain and Bob Hilliard © 1951
Walt Disney Music Company. Used by permission.

Printed in Hong Kong

First Edition

1 3 5 7 9 10 8 6 4 2

Library of Congress Cataloging-in-Publication Data on file.

Book design by Christine Kettner

Hand lettering by Leah Palmer Preiss

ISBN 978-1-4231-0728-6

Alice in Wonderland

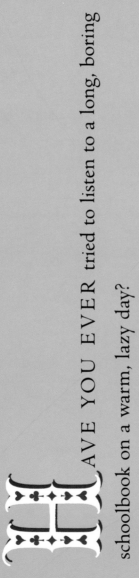

HAVE YOU EVER tried to listen to a long, boring schoolbook on a warm, lazy day?

And have you ever wondered why anyone would make a book so boring?

Then you are just like Alice.

Because that is exactly what happened to her.

As Alice sat warm and sleepy, trying to listen to her sister read and daydreaming of how she would make books much more interesting and how she would make a world with less sense and more nonsense and how she might or might not make a chain of daisies . . . a White Rabbit ran by.

Now, Alice didn't think it was strange to see a rabbit.

But she did think it was very strange to see this rabbit take out a watch and to hear him say, "I'm late. I'm late. For a very important date!"

Which is why Alice, curious, jumped up and followed the White Rabbit right into his rabbit hole.

Which is how Alice, very curious, found herself suddenly falling . . . and falling . . . and falling . . . and f a l l i n g .

The rabbit hole was either very deep, or she was falling very slowly, because as Alice fell, she had time to review most of her spelling words (72% correct), recite two poems (poorly), and say all of her 7 times tables (all wrong) before landing with a gentle t h u m p.

ALICE saw the White Rabbit disappear through a tiny door.

"Curiouser and curiouser," said Alice, who was so surprised she forgot how to speak correct English.

She was much too big to fit through the rabbit-size door. So she followed the directions on a bottle:

DRINK ME.

Alice shrunk down to just the right size and grabbed the doorknob.

L o c k e d .

The key was, of course, on a now-giant tabletop way above her head.

THE WAVES of giant tears washed Alice ashore and into the woods.

Something wiggled in the bushes. It must be the White Rabbit, thought Alice.

But it wasn't. It was two odd fellows named Tweedledee and Tweedledum.

They didn't look at all helpful, but to be polite, Alice introduced herself.

"My name is Alice," said You-Know-Who. "And I'm following a White Rabbit."

"She's curious," said Tweedledee.

"The Oysters were curious, too," said Tweedledum. "And you remember what happened to them."

"What *did* happen to the Oysters?" asked Alice.

Tweedledee and Tweedledum happily recited their poem about the Curious Oysters. The Oysters were invited to dinner by the Walrus. But they ended up *being* the dinner.

"That's a very sad story," said Alice.

"But it has a good moral," said Tweedledee.

"If you are an Oyster," said Alice.

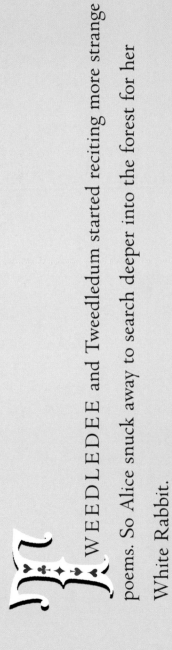

TWEEDLEDEE and Tweedledum started reciting more strange poems. So Alice snuck away to search deeper into the forest for her White Rabbit.

A loaf of Bread-and-Butter Flies flew lazily overhead. Alice spotted Crab-Grass, and a tiny horse with wings and rockers.

"A Rocking-Horse Fly!" said Alice.

"Naturally," said the rose. (At least Alice thought it was the rose.)

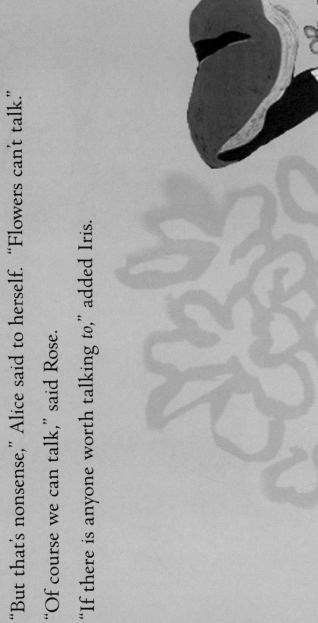

"But that's nonsense," Alice said to herself. "Flowers can't talk."

"Of course we can talk," said Rose.

"If there is anyone worth talking *to*," added Iris.

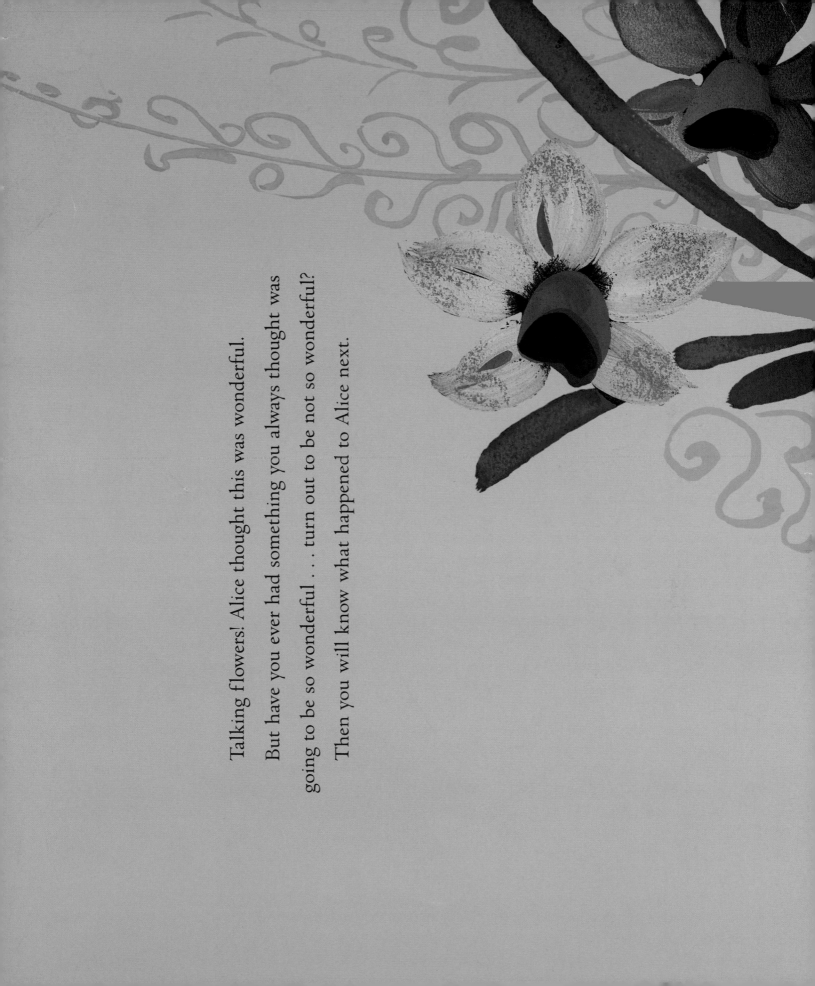

Talking flowers! Alice thought this was wonderful.

But have you ever had something you always thought was

going to be so wonderful . . . turn out to be not so wonderful?

Then you will know what happened to Alice next.

The flowers talked. The flowers sang.

Then the flowers started asking questions.

"What kind of garden do you come from?"

"What species are you?"

Then the flowers started yelling.

"She's a weed!"

The nasty flowers chased Alice out of their garden.

A LICE ran and ran until she was right back where she started—lost.

Alice was just beginning to worry when she saw a toothy smile floating in a tree.

The smile turned into a Cheshire Cat and said, "If you'd really like to know . . . he went that way."

"Who did?" asked Alice.

"The White Rabbit," said the Cat.

"He did?"

"He did what?"

"Went that way."

"Who did?"

"The White Rabbit!" said Alice.

"What rabbit?" asked the grinning Cat.

"Ooooooh!" said Alice.

"Though if I were looking for a White Rabbit," said the Cat, "I'd ask the Mad Hatter."

"But I don't want to go among mad people," said Alice.

"Oh, you can't help that. Most everyone is mad here." The Cheshire Cat laughed.

Then he disappeared.

ALICE found the Mad Hatter and the March Hare having a tea party to celebrate their unbirthdays.

The Mad Hatter sang, "Now statistics prove, prove that you've one birthday. But there are three hundred and sixty-four UNbirthdays!"

"Why, today is my unbirthday, too," said Alice.

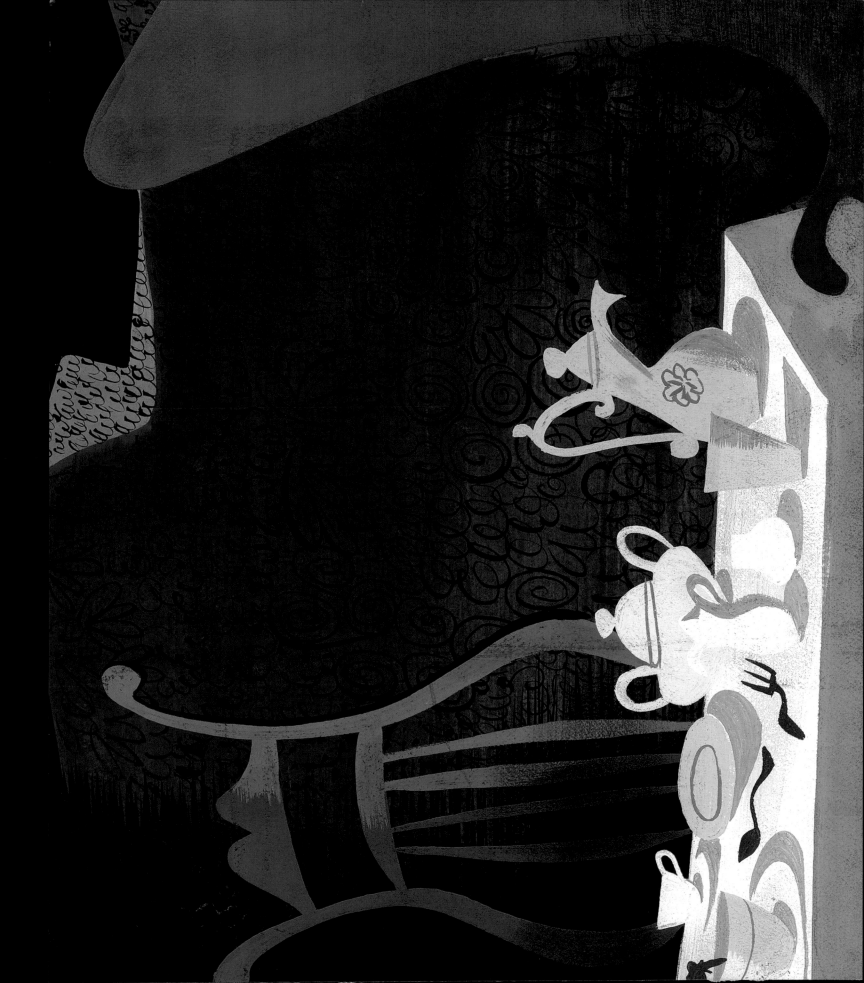

The Mad Hatter and March Hare cheered.

They poured more tea everywhere.

A little sleeping Dormouse woke up and joined the celebration by reciting a poem that sounded almost familiar . . . but not quite right:

Twinkle, twinkle, little bat,

How I wonder what you're at.

Up above the world you fly,

Like a tea tray in the sky.

The Dormouse fell back asleep.

Alice thought this tea party was too curious, even for her. So when the March Hare asked her to stay for more tea, Alice answered, "I just haven't the time."

"The TIME? The TIME? Who's got the TIME?" yelled the Mad Hatter.

And like an answer to the question, a small figure hopped through the hedge, looking at his watch, saying, "No time. No time. I'm late, I'm late, I'm late."

"The White Rabbit!" cried Alice.

The Mad Hatter grabbed the White Rabbit's watch and held it to his ear. "No wonder you're late. This clock is exactly two days slow."

The Hatter and the Hare popped open the White Rabbit's watch.

They buttered the gears. They sugared the springs. They strawberry-jammed the wheels.

Tick-tock, tick-tick, tock-tock—BLAM!

Time exploded.

The Mad Hatter and the March Hare picked up the White Rabbit and heaved him over the hedge.

"This is the stupidest tea party I've been to in all my life," said Alice.

And it was.

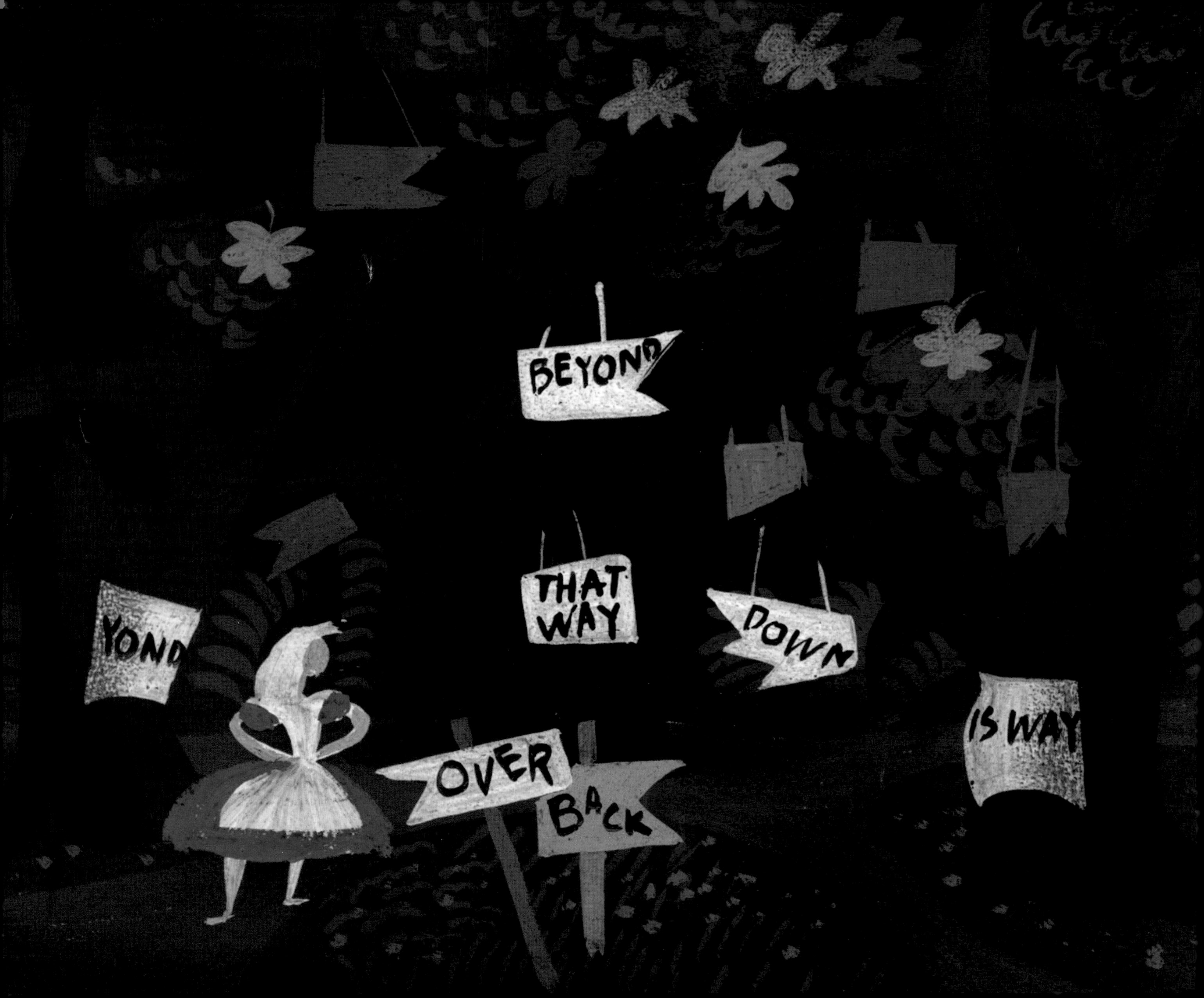
BEYOND
YOND
THAT WAY
DOWN
IS WAY
OVER
BACK

ALICE ran to catch up to the White Rabbit.
And I'm sure you know what happened next. She couldn't find him.

"I've had enough nonsense," said Alice. "I'm going straight home."
But when she read the signs to find her way, they were no help at all.

Alice grew sad, then worried, then frightened. She cried to herself just a little
bit, missing her home and even her boring schoolbook.

The moon, curved like a smile in the darkening sky, rose overhead.

"I want to go home," said Alice. "But I can't find my way."

"Naturally," said the moon, turning into the smile of the Cheshire Cat. "That's because all ways are the Queen's ways."

The Cat opened a door in a nearby tree to show Alice the castle of the Queen of Hearts.

Alice, curious as ever, did exactly what you would do.

She made her way to the castle.

There she saw three gardeners painting a white rosebush red.

"The Queen she likes them red," said the Three of Clubs. "If she saw white instead, she'd raise a fuss, and each of us would quickly lose his head."

"Oh, dear," said Alice. "Then let me help you."

But before Alice and the gardeners could paint the last rose red, the royal horns sounded.

"The Queen!" yelled the Three of Clubs.

Cards came marching from every direction.

Clubs, Spades, Hearts, and Diamonds.

Ones, Twos, Threes, and Fours.

Fives, Sixes, Sevens, and Eights.

Nines, Tens, and Jacks.

And almost late, almost late, for a very important date

(but just in time to do his job) came, at last, Guess Who?

"The White Rabbit," said Alice.

The White Rabbit blew his horn and announced, "Her Royal Majesty— the Queen of Hearts!"

Alice had always thought it would be so wonderful to meet a queen.

But you remember how some of those "so wonderful" things turn out.

"Who's been painting my roses red?" yelled the Queen. "Off with their heads!"

Alice began to politely explain, "I'm trying to find my way home."

"*Your way*?! All ways are *my* ways!" yelled the Queen.

And you won't be surprised to hear what she yelled next.

"Off with her head!"

The cards swarmed Alice.

Alice didn't think she should be afraid of a deck of cards.

But she was rather attached to her head.

Alice saw the White Rabbit run.

So Alice ran, too.

Alice ran back through the hedges, back past the Mad Hatter and March Hare,

back past Tweedledee and Tweedledum.

"Off with her head!" yelled the Queen of Hearts.

Alice found the tiny door. L o c k e d .

"I simply must get out!" said Alice.

"But you are o u t . . . s i d e ," said the door.

Alice looked through the keyhole. The door was right.

She *was* outside, fast asleep, dreaming under a tree on a warm, lazy day.

The angry cards and their mean Queen charged.

"*Alice, please wake up,*" Alice called to herself.

"*Alice, please wake up,*" Alice heard her sister call.

And suddenly, Alice was awake, outside, and no longer in her Wonderland.

Alice tried to tell her sister all about the Mad Hatter and unbirthdays and the Cheshire Cat and the Queen of Hearts, and especially, the White Rabbit.

But you know how it is with some people.

Sometimes they get too grown up to understand.

"Come along," said Alice's sister. "It's time for tea."

Alice thought about her Wonderland and her White Rabbit.

She decided she would remember them for all time, no matter how grown up she might ever be.

AND THEN she went for tea.

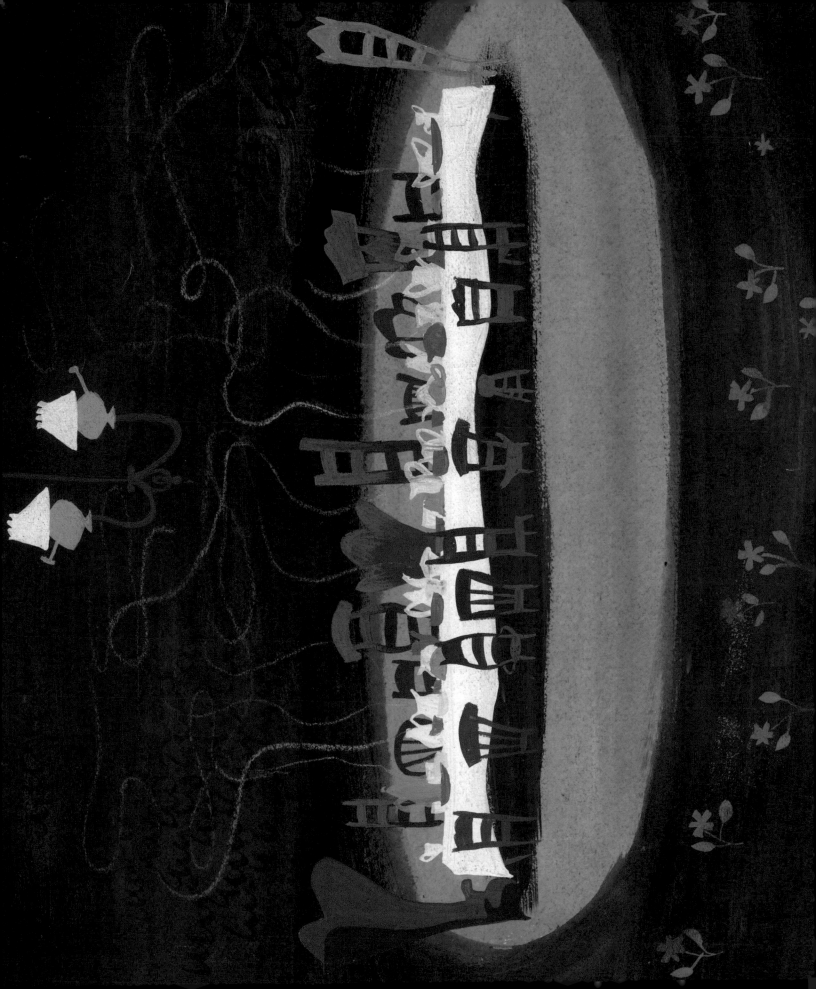

The End

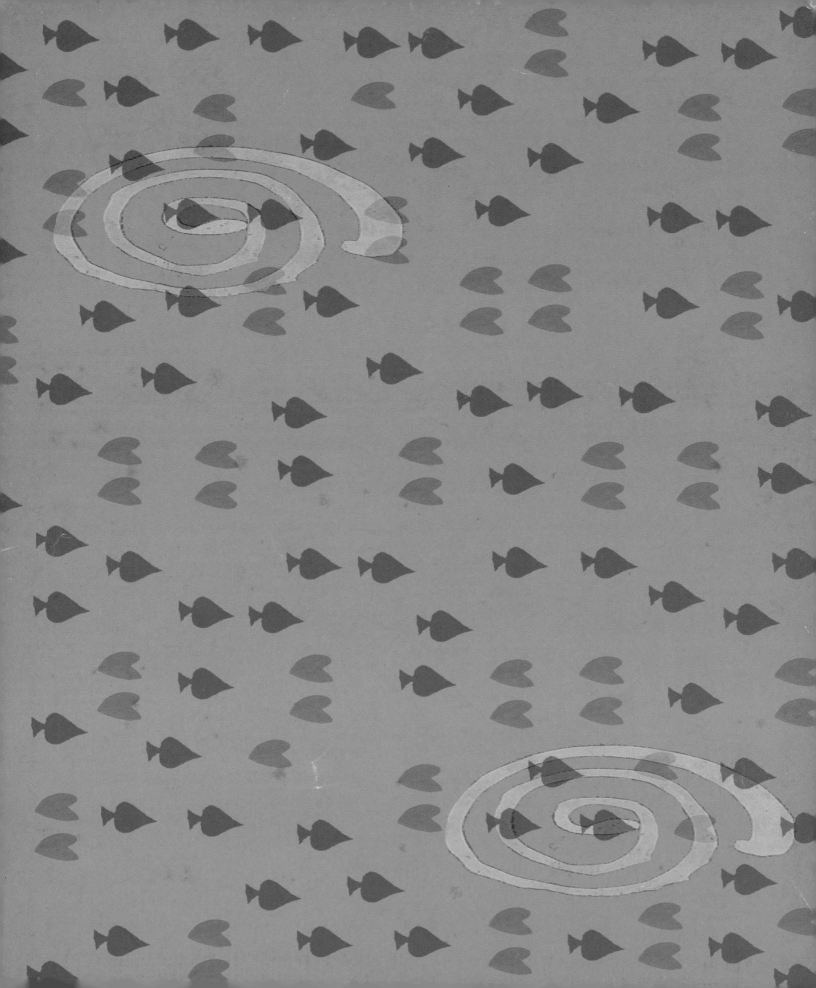